Things that Make Me Happy

By Sarah Mazor

Illustrator: BTween Animation

Thank you for purchasing

Things *that* **make me happy**

Please join the kids and me
and play the Happy Game.
To share with me what makes
you happy, send your eMail to:
HappyMorejoy@MazorBooks.com

Remember! It is always good to
greet all with a smile.
Love,
Miss Happy

Author's Note

Happy children fare better socially and academically. Happy children also feel better about themselves because happiness, which is an emotional and mental state of well-being, contributes to a healthier perception of the self and enhances self-confidence.

Life, however, is not always cheery and fun. Things happen that sadden us, adults and children alike. And it is okay to be sad and even healthy to cry and allow time for sadness, so long as it is not for a prolonged period of time. When sadness lasts too long we must do something about it.

There are different ways to cheer ourselves and others and it is a good idea to do so. One of the most effective methods to cure the blues - a technique that works for all age groups - is thinking happy thoughts and then expressing them vocally.

In *Things that Make Me Happy* preschool kids chase sadness away with happy thoughts they say out loud.

Enjoy!

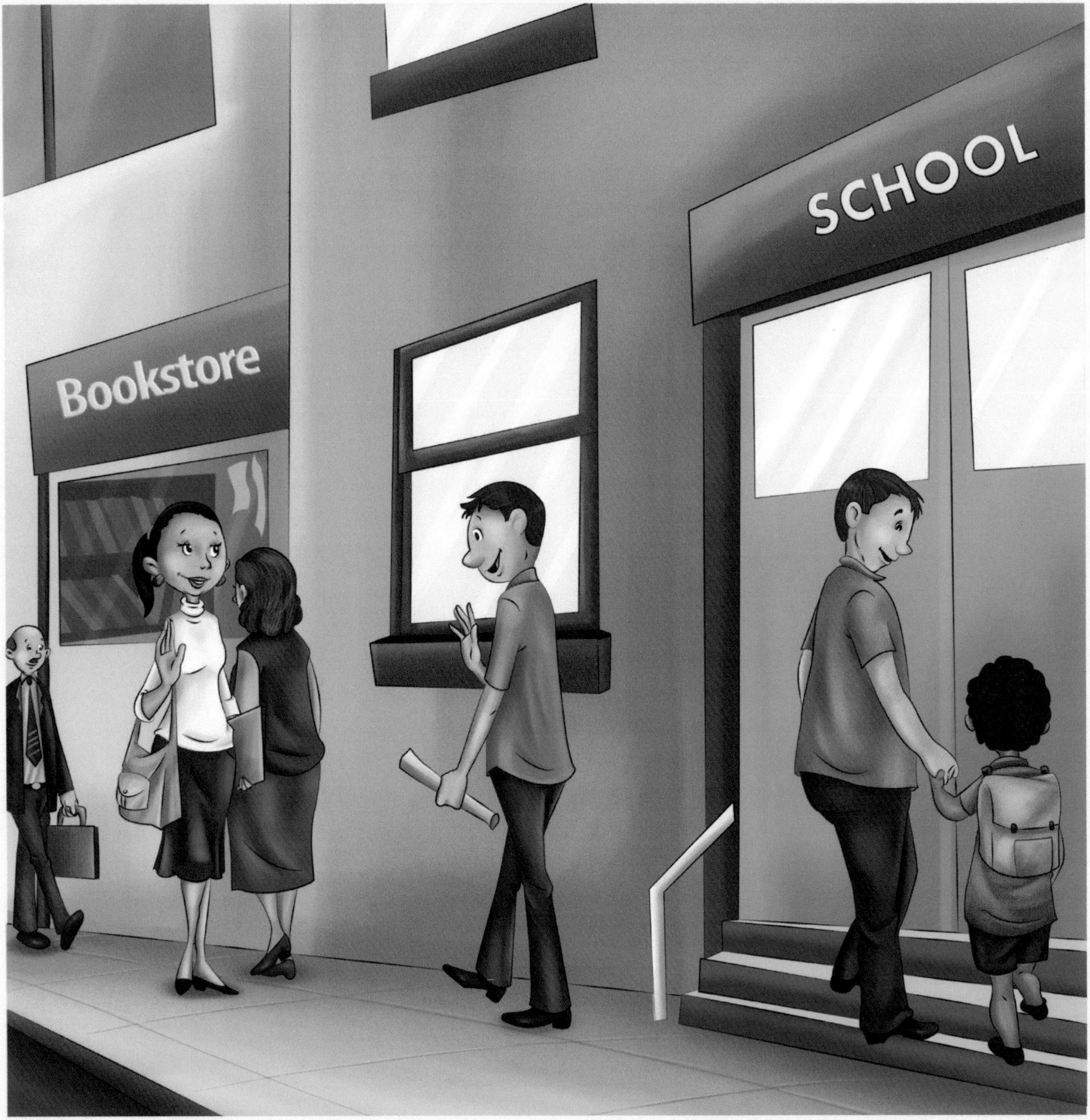
Bookstore
SCHOOL

Miss Happy Morejoy was everyone's favorite preschool teacher in a little town called Celebration. Miss Happy Morejoy, just like her name suggests, brought happiness and more joy to everyone.

Miss Happy was always happy to see the children in her class. She smiled at them a lot, encouraged them to do well and always celebrated their success.

That is why everyone was surprised one morning when Miss Happy came to school and sat down at her desk without her usual bright smile. Miss Happy looked sad.

"Miss Happy," cried all the children in her class. "Why are you sad?"

"I am a little sad because I had to say goodbye to my beloved dog, Old Sam," said Miss Happy. "Old Sam is now in doggie heaven."

"That is so sad," agreed the children. They all knew Old Sam and they all loved him a whole lot.

"We will miss good Old Sam," said Jonathan. The kids nodded their heads and they all looked sad too.

But then little Hannah said, "Miss Happy, you always told us that Old Sam was the happiest dog around."

"Yes, he was," said Miss Happy, her face thoughtful. "Old Sam was always happy."

"Old Sam had a long happy life and he was very old," said Jacob. "I think he would like us to be happy too."

"You are right, Jacob," said Miss Happy. "Old Sam loved happiness and smiles."

Miss Happy looked around the class. She saw the sad faces and realized something had to be done.

"I know what we should do today," said Miss Happy. "Let us play the Happy Game. I am sure that will cheer us all up."

"Yay," said all the children.

"Come on then," said Miss Happy as she got off her chair, went to the middle of the room and sat on the floor. "Come on and join me."

Once the children settled in a circle around Miss Happy, she asked, "Who wants to begin?"

"I will," said Suzie.

"Wonderful," said Miss Happy. "And then everyone will have a chance to share their happy thoughts."

Suzie thought for a moment and then she began:

Things that make me happy,
Are things that warm my heart.
Like Mommy's kiss and Daddy's hug,
Best way for a day to start.

Miss Happy smiled at Suzie and said, "I agree. It is wonderful to start each day with loving kisses and warm hugs."

Bobby, who sat across from Suzie, was next to share with Miss Happy and the other kids.

Things that make me happy,
Are stacked up in a pile.
It is books I love and that is why,
I am a bibliophile.

"Bibliophile is a big word, Bobby," said Miss Happy.

"Yes, I know," said Bobby proudly. "Bibliophile means a lover of books.".

"Indeed it does," said Miss Happy and smiled some more.

"It is your turn, Emma," said Miss Happy.
"Tell us what brings you joy?"

Emma thought for a moment and then she said:

Things that make me happy,
Are colorful and bright.
A hot air balloon, a rainbow,
And a multi-colored kite.

"Wonderful, Emma," said Miss Happy and clapped her hands with joy. "I love colors too. Bright ones and joyful ones make me smile."

"Jonathan, you go now," said Miss Happy. Jonathan smiled and then he began:

Things that make me happy,
Are fun and joyful games.
Like playing hide and seek,
With Erica and James.

"I think games are fun too, Jonathan," said Miss Happy. "Playing with friends is so very enjoyable."

"And now it is Hannah's turn," said Jonathan.

"Indeed it is," said Miss Happy and turned her attention to Hannah.

Hannah stood up and said:

Things that make me happy,
Are soft and also fluffy.
That's why I love to pet,
My little kitten, Buffy.

"Yes, Hannah," said Miss Happy softly. "It is nice to have furry friends."

"Alright then, Jacob," said Miss Happy.
"Now you tell us what makes you smile."
"Okay," said Jacob. "Here I go."

Things that make me happy,
Are cool and creamy and good.
Like chocolate ice cream on a cone,
I'd have some now, if I could.

"I love ice cream too," said Miss Happy.
And all the kids agreed.

"My turn," said Katie and started to laugh.

"Yes, go on," said Miss Happy her smile wide.

Katie made a funny face and then she said:

Things that make me happy,
Are things that make me laugh.
Like a funny show, a goofy face,
A silly word or a foolish gaffe.

"A foolish gaffe," exclaimed Miss Happy. "What a wonderful way to say a clumsy mistake. Foolish gaffes make me laugh too."

"And now Zach," said Miss Happy, "it is your turn."

"I need to think," said Zach. "So many of the things that make me happy have already been said." He thought for a while longer.

"Oh, I know!" Said Zach and then he began:

Things that make me happy,
Are in the music store.
Like pianos, guitars and trumpets,
And flutes and much, much more.

"Ah, yes," said Miss Happy. "Music makes me happy too. It makes me want to dance."

"So let us all dance," said Bobby.

"Great idea," said Miss Happy. "Come on kids, let us all dance!"

Miss Happy turned the music on and everyone joined in. After a while all were tired and sat back down to rest.

"Miss Happy," said Zach. "Please tell us what makes you happy."

"Yes, Zach," said Miss Happy. "It is my turn and I do want to share with you kids what makes me happy."

Miss Happy smiled broadly at the children.
She then looked at the picture on her desk
and said:

There are lots of things that make me smile,
Like rain and sun and stars up high.
And flowers and kittens and bunnies too,
And watching birds and airplanes fly.

Yet more than all, I realize now,
How blessed I truly am.
To be with you, such lovely kids,
Remembering Old Sam.

Miss Happy looked around the room at the smiling faces and continued:

And so we will conclude today,
With a lesson, so worthwhile.
No matter what, it's always good,
To greet all with a smile.

The happy children clapped their hands. Then all of them rushed to Miss Happy for their daily group hug.

Now it is your turn!

What makes you happy?

Check out the MazorBooks Library

Children's Books with Good Values

www.MazorBooks.com

www.mazorbooks.wordpress.com

www.facebook.com/mazorbooks

CPSIA information can be obtained
at www.ICGtesting.com
Printed in the USA
LVIC06n1734140514
385782LV00007B/183

* 9 7 8 1 4 9 7 5 5 0 0 6 3 *